Dead Heart Longing

Fizza Younis

Copyright © 2024 Fizza Younis

All rights reserved

The characters and events portrayed in this book are fictitious. Any similarity to real persons, living or dead, is coincidental and not intended by the author.

No part of this book may be reproduced, stored in a retrieval system, or transmitted in any form or by any means, electronic, mechanical, photocopying, recording, or otherwise, without express written permission of the publisher.

Cover design by: Fizza Younis

To that one person, who knows me
the best and loves me still

CONTENTS

Title Page

Copyright

Dedication

A Lost Soul   1

Past Haunts the Future   7

Nothing Lasts Forever   13

Seeing the Unseen   19

Truth Within the Lies   24

Be Still My Dead Heart   30

The Knots of Fate   36

Journey to the Past   42

Much is Lost in Time   48

Back to the Beginning   54

Dead Hearts Don't Beat   57

The Cruel Lies   63

The Nagi Princess   67

The Mystery in Mayhem	73
The Untold Tale	79
Coming Back to Life	84
One Last Battle	89
That Fateful Night	96
The Old Magic	100
Reunited Once More	105
Afterword	107
About The Author	109
Books by This Author	111

A LOST SOUL

The castle stood on the highest hill in a valley surrounded by the mighty Himalayas. From its towers, in all four directions, you could see tiny houses and huts stretched as far as your eyes could roam uninterrupted by nature. Though calling it a castle would probably be wrong, it was more of a ruin of one. Yet, its vastness would leave you in awe.

On the outside, vines crawled on every wall. Shrubs and wildflowers overran the grounds. Trees of silver fir and blue pine scattered across the uneven landscape. Broken windows shuddered with each gust of wind. And the inside was bare of any furniture or sign that humans ever lived there. Cobwebs hung from walls, and dust coated the cabinets. Shadows lurked in the corners and monsters seemed to peek from each dark nook.

Locals avoided it, fearful of the ghosts and goblins that haunted the empty structure—a shell of its past glory. As magnificent as the sun in the sky on a cloudless day, once upon a time, the grandeur of its halls was unparalleled. Now, a husk of its former self, it was still standing. That alone was something of a marvel.

Back in the day, tourists frequented the place, but then it was deemed unstable and unsafe for viewing. She was a brave girl who dared to darken its corridors, for no one else bothered with the falling skeleton of an ancient castle. At least, not in the past decade or so.

"Look, you must come and see it for yourself," she was talking into the phone. "This place needs saving. It's a national treasure. Seriously, it might be the oldest standing building in the Himalayas. Imagine the benefits if we succeeded in getting it declared as such."

Her excitement grew with each word she uttered and her green eyes shone. Whether that too was a result of her eagerness or because of the afternoon sun, he couldn't tell. Everything about her was illuminated and to his eyes, she seemed like a phantom. Maybe he conjured her up with sheer will. No, he wasn't *that* imaginative. He quickly discarded the idea because she was real. More so than him.

It wasn't the first time an outsider came to the valley and fell in love with its history. Unfortunately, all previous efforts to get the place status of a historical site failed. It would take too many resources to restore the castle and make it safe enough for human viewing. It was practically falling apart, which made it dangerous, especially if you considered its location—at the edge of a steep hill with at least a hundred feet fall on three sides. And only one travelable dirt road leading in or out of its giant front gates.

"Don't you trust my judgment?" she said to whoever was on the other end. She waited for their response before continuing, "Times are different now. I'm sure it's possible. In this day and age, what isn't? We can even turn it into one of the hottest tourist destinations."

Whatever the other person said satisfied her. "Okay, that's settled then. I'll see you next week." Putting her phone back in her bag, she turned a corner and found herself in front of a doorway that barely reached her shoulders. She was a tall woman but that wasn't why the door seemed dwarfed in front of her. This particular door led to a small room, which in turn led to the dungeons. And it was deliberately constructed to make sure the entrants would lower their heads, thus, ruling out sneak attacks.

She stood there for a long moment, admiring the carvings on its wooden frame, still as sturdy as ever before. *'Not everything decayed at the same rate,'* he mused. The invaders who came along the road of time might have stolen the jewels and gems, but the wooden door and window frames with intricate designs were no less precious. They were a testament to its past splendor. Dulled with dirt, they bespoke the craftmanship that existed hundreds of years ago.

He kept following her as she walked around and observed every nook of the castle's main building. Meanwhile, he observed her. She was the first person he had seen in centuries. At least, that's what it felt like to him. Time was no longer relevant to his existence. Even though she couldn't see or hear him, just watching her admiring his home was entertainment enough. Her presence in the ruins of *his* castle fascinated him. How long had he craved human interaction, and how many nights had he wished to gaze upon another face—any face, let alone a pretty one. She was his dream come true and his heart's deepest desire.

It wouldn't be easy to understand his reaction if you hadn't roamed the vacant corridors and halls of an abandoned, rundown castle for centuries. If you didn't know what it felt like to go from one empty room to another when you can't even sleep to seek a few hours of reprieve in your dreams. Unable to leave the place and cursed to remain invisible to anyone who came to study its ancient walls, Gesar was truly lost and utterly alone.

Some might consider immortality a blessing, but he knew it for the curse it was. Destined to walk on the earth in solitude, having no one to love or cherish, he spent one day at a time while avoiding the thoughts of what was to come. At first, he hoped to find peace in his pointless existence, but centuries of loneliness drained him of all his hopes. The only thing he felt now was a burning desire for revenge.

He didn't remember much from the time when he was alive. His sole vivid memory was of his gruesome death. Even after all these years, he could still feel the blade of a sword piercing his heart and the touch of its hilt clutched in his hands as he fell backward, down the hill, from the castle's tallest tower, into the dark abyss below. At least, he didn't remember hitting the rocks. Perhaps, he died before he hit the ground.

Gesar could vaguely recall running through these halls as a child and a sense of belonging was his only clue that this palace was once home to him. He had forgotten the faces of his family and friends, but he must have had those. Sometimes, when he thought hard enough about the past, he felt a sense of betrayal choking him and a longing to make someone pay for it.

"Shit!"

The curse brought his attention back to the woman in front of him. She sucked at her index finger. A splinter must have pierced it. Gesar felt a hollow ache in his heart, and a tear rolled down his ghostly cheek. Why he reacted to her discomfort in such an intense way was a mystery to him, but he had an uncanny feeling their paths were about to entangle in a way neither the god of mountains nor the goddess of fates could explain.

PAST HAUNTS THE FUTURE

Even if you didn't think about it, even when you didn't plan for it, the future happened anyway. It's impossible to isolate it from your past because everything that happened until then would determine what would happen next. That's what Gesar always believed and why he remained restless.

Without unraveling his past, he couldn't begin to think about his future. Though he might not have one, considering he was nothing but a ghost. Yet, he could never accept that fact. There must be some logic behind his existence. Otherwise, why would he be cursed to roam undead or dead—he was still not sure—instead of moving on to the afterlife?

The problem isn't that it didn't last. The problem is that you thought it would. When has anything lasted forever? I'm sorry you believed love would endure. Your faith in human emotion was misplaced. It's as fickle as humans themselves. Someday you will forgive yourself for being naïve, but I understand it won't be for a while. If possible, do forgive me, for I am but human.

Gesar fell to his knees as the words resonated in his head. The voice was unfamiliar, but the words weren't. Someone had said that to him. Was it in this lifetime or another? Slowly he stood up. Unnerved, he tried to focus on the woman standing in front of him. She faced him, but instead of looking at him, she stared out the window behind him.

A memory resurfaced as he stared into her eyes, but this one wasn't painful. When he was alive, he had once stared into those same eyes and confessed his love to the woman they belonged to—a woman who was the mirror image of the one standing there. If he hadn't already, he would definitely have stopped breathing then.

Nostalgia washed over him, and he wished she could see him. If only he could speak to her. He would ask her who she was and why she was in his past. And what of the future?

Alas, he couldn't talk to her. All he could do was to keep looking at her face, trying to drink in every line that appeared on it as she thought about something.

I'm not the same person you knew and loved. Too much time has passed. I waited for you for twelve years. But you were gone, and I was all alone. Much has changed, my love. Please, don't blame me. Blame the gods if you must. Blame the war that kept you away from me. The battlefield called to you more than my love ever could.

The words echoed in his mind as yet another memory returned to haunt him. They were bitter and laced with hurt and anger. She might be in his arms, but he couldn't find the love he sought in her eyes. The woman he gave his heart to forgot he even existed.

He wanted to curse and shake her. How could she forget him so soon? What were twelve years when they had promised each other eternity? For the first time in his life, he truly wished he wasn't a king, and the fate of his kingdom didn't rest on his shoulders. Then he wouldn't have needed to fight for his people, and he wouldn't have lost his love amidst the chaos of battle cries and bloody bodies.

We can fight fate all we want, but it will do us no good. Perhaps, the gods didn't write a happy ending for us. It might be the only story we are destined to live. Can't you accept the will of god and not demand from me something I can no longer give you?

Had he been a demanding husband? Did he ask for too much from his queen? The past and present blurred, making it impossible for him to tell the difference. On instinct, he reached out to touch the woman's face, but his fingers went right through it, reminding him of the horrible reality of his situation. Could ghosts go mad? Had he lost his mind and started dreaming up things that weren't real?

The woman had cringed and closed her eyes. But she couldn't see him. Could she? Trying to calm himself, he looked away. She was a stranger, and he had never met her before. *'She isn't my queen,'* he repeated to himself as if that would make him forget the pain of rejection. But she wasn't the one who rejected him.

Before then, he hadn't experienced anything like this, and his past had always been elusive. No wonder he couldn't follow her after that. She would leave soon, anyway. There was no point in getting himself emotional when he couldn't do anything about it. After all, she couldn't even see him let alone talk to him. If he had any questions, they would remain unanswered. What was even the point of obsessing over a living breathing person when he was already dead?

Gesar never truly believed in the gods, but if the goddess of fates existed, she must be laughing at his predicament. Or perhaps, it was her doing. Whatever might be the case, he wasn't about to start praying to someone who left him to mourn his death alone.

He didn't mind the memories as much as their timing. The day started well when a beautiful woman visited his home. He had admired her tall, willowy figure as she fearlessly went up the stairs of his favorite tower. A bit foolish, but he admired her courage.

The tower faced the east, and he often went up there to welcome the sun. The sight of the rising sun, peeking from behind the mountains, was still his favorite thing in the world. It didn't matter how often he witnessed it. There was also something soothing about it. No matter what happened in the world, the sun never forgot to rise. Whether you were there to greet it or not, it would make an appearance. It might hide behind the clouds sometimes, but it would never abandon earth. The surety of that grounded him.

The woman in question hadn't been scared of the height or the unstable steps. She braved them and went up the tower to look around. He liked that about her. Forgetting everything else, he basked in her very presence. But then, the unwanted memories of his long-lost queen left a bad taste in his mouth. He couldn't tell if they were real or just his imagination, but they distracted him from the woman right in front of him.

Soon, the night would crawl in, the woman would leave, and he would find a cozy corner in the garden to sit and reminisce about the day. He wouldn't think about the memories of the past. He would only think about the present and the possibility that this woman might return. From the conversation he overheard, this might not be her only visit to his castle. That thought brought a smile to his face.

NOTHING LASTS FOREVER

When you were betrayed or left behind by someone you loved, you would forget all the good times you had with them. As painful as it might be, you would only remember the moment they broke your heart. That single moment would stay with you forever, while many other happy moments would not. It was hard to remember the closeness you once shared with someone who was now practically a stranger.

Then, was it strange that he forgot about the time they were inseparable? Staring up at the stars, Gesar recalled the woman who once shared the heavenly sight with him. Reclining on a divan on one of the balconies, they used to talk about everything and nothing. In those moments, he knew life couldn't get any better, and he was right.

△△△

Startled, Gesar opened his eyes and gawked at the flying squirrel scurrying away. As soon as he realized he had been asleep, his world tilted on its axis once again.

The first time it had happened was when he had opened his eyes and found that no one could see or hear him. The realization of becoming a ghost had taken him many years to accept. In those early days, he had tried everything he could to attract anyone's attention, but nothing had worked. Over the centuries, he had watched history play out in front of his eyes, and yet, he wasn't an active participant.

Today was the second time something shook his reality. He fell asleep, and not only that, but he had been dreaming. Now that he was up, the dream faded away, but the feeling of warmth and love stayed with him.

Gesar had never felt like he truly belonged anywhere, but the castle had been his home for many centuries. And now, for the first time, it was utterly foreign to him. The walls stared at him as if telling him to leave. The pillars made him feel like a stranger.

Something wasn't right, but he couldn't put his finger on it. The overwhelming sensation of discontent troubled him, and he feared he might drown in his misery. After so many years, why was he no longer welcome within these walls? What had changed? Regardless of how much he thought about it, he couldn't figure it out. All he knew was he must leave and soon. Where would he go, though? Where *could* he go?

Once a fearless king, Gesar was too scared to leave the castle. *'I can't leave this place,'* he reminded himself. *'I have never been able to.'* And it was the truth. His every attempt at leaving the place ended with him in the dungeons and unable to move for days. Sometimes even weeks. Whichever god decided to play a joke on him by bringing his soul back didn't want him to leave these ruins. He had even tried jumping from the towers and met with failure. After exhausting all his resources, he concluded he couldn't leave the castle and should wander within these walls aimlessly.

Now, his dead heart wanted him to leave. Tentatively, he took a step forward and passed over the threshold of the gate. Nothing happened. He stood there, still for a long time, waiting to be thrown into the darkest dungeons, but that didn't happen. Taking another step, he crossed over the threshold and was outside.

Before he could relish his newfound freedom, he was thrown backward. Instead of ending in the dungeon, he ended up in the great hall.

'Ouch!' he cried out as a stabbing pain assaulted his senses. Was he hurt? But that was impossible. Yet, his ribs ached from where he had

collided with the stone pillar with enough force to have his ribs broken. Ghosts shouldn't feel pain. Confused, he tried to wrap his mind around what was happening to him, when a familiar voice reached his ears.

The woman paused in the middle of her conversation and glanced toward him. For a millisecond he thought she saw him, but then, she continued talking. "You're late, and I'm quickly losing my patience." She didn't sound happy with the person on the other end of the phone.

A minute later, she walked out of the hall with her phone still pressed to her ears. The woman must love talking into that piece of technology.

Even in isolation, his existence wasn't one of ignorance. He knew what it was from a few trespassers who had wandered into his territory over the years. People seemed to love that thing.

Up until a century ago, this place bustled with life. It might not have been the great kingdom it once was, but his descendants ruled with the same pride and sense of duty. Then the land was divided, and all the tribes dissolved to become part of democratic governments. A concept Gesar would never understand.

The world was different from what it used to be, and the stories of great kings and queens like him became legends that later became myths. Much was lost, even if much else was gained in the process.

"I didn't want to say anything, but how long will you keep following me?"

Gesar had followed the woman, but it took him a while to realize she wasn't holding a phone and was actually speaking to him. She looked directly at him and raised her eyebrows as if demanding an answer.

He was speechless. "Can you see me?" he croaked at last. His voice was hoarse with emotions more than the lack of use.

There was something regal in the way she stood there, tall and confident. Her steady gaze upon him gave him an uncanny feeling that nothing remained hidden from her scrutiny—as if she could see into his soul. Though, technically, he was nothing but a soul. He wondered how she could see him when no one else ever had.

She seemed unfazed by his presence as if it was something normal. "Yes, I can see you. I have always been able to see ghosts. I wanted to ignore you at first. That day too, you kept following me around. Why?"

The answer should be simple, but Gesar didn't know what to say. He was still reeling from the fact that someone could see him and hear his voice. "I—" he began and stopped. "You," he tried again but couldn't say more than a word.

"I'm sorry," she said. "I sometimes forget that seers are rare. Is it your first time talking to someone?" This time her tone was gentle as if coaxing a child.

He wanted to say so much. His heart would be pounding in his chest if it still could. If he had been alive, tears of joy would've rolled down his cheeks. Who knew this moment—in the centuries of existence—would become his most cherished? That woman was his destiny. He was more certain of it than he had ever been of anything. His story might yet get another conclusion.

SEEING THE UNSEEN

Not many things unsettled Nur, but a ghost following her every move was definitely flustering. In her experience, most ghosts were trapped between the worlds, which makes it impossible for them to move on or reincarnate. Usually, it resulted from a curse or some unfinished business. Most of these ghosts would be restless and aggressive. This one, though, showed no signs of hostility. She doubted he even wanted anything from her. Or else, he would've tried to get her attention instead of following her quietly.

Not once had he tried to talk to her, which meant he hadn't guessed she was a seer. But why did he follow her around then? The thought troubled her a little, but more troubling was how he looked at her—as if he was dying of thirst and she was the last drop of water on earth. Even now, his gaze held a longing that broke the heart she always claimed she didn't have. Talk about confusing.

"You seem quite at home here. What's your deal, anyway?" she asked the ghost in question. He wasn't a tall man, and she was tall for a woman, which meant they were almost the same height. Standing like this, facing one another, they could see directly into each other's eyes.

"I... I..." He stuttered at first, but then somewhat unsteadily, he said, "Yes, because this is my home."

"Your home?" Nur observed him closely and noticed he wasn't old and probably died in his early thirties. His black, straight hair reached his waist and hung in a loose ponytail. His robes were traditional Tibetan; full-length cross-over, tied with a sash and had a high collar. Its azure color adorned with intricate green and gold patterns looked pleasing. Strange how it wasn't the first thing she noticed about him, but then, she had been too mesmerized by his eyes to notice anything else. Now that she paid attention, she could ascertain from his attire that he had been dead for quite a while. Her best guess was a century or so ago.

"Yes, I was born here. And I died here, too."

'Ah, more than a century ago then,' she thought. "Anyway, let's get back to my original question. Why are you following me?"

This time when he spoke his voice was steady. "No one has entered the castle in decades, and I can't leave." He paused and said, "So, I just wanted human interaction. By the way, are you even allowed to be here?"

That didn't perturb Nur. She had come across enough ghosts to know how much they liked to be in the company of the living. Early in life, she learned to pretend as if she didn't see them. Ghosts were rarely dangerous, but they could be a pest sometimes. If they realized you could see or hear them, they would attach themselves to you like your shadow, and you wouldn't have a moment of peace after that.

Nur Bakht came from a long line of seers with the sight passed down from woman to woman. Her grandmother used it to help people by playing mediator between the living and the dead. She used to say that the purpose of their gift was to guide the lost to find their way home, the cursed to undo their curses, and the burdened to unload their burdens. But Nur's mother was a modern woman. She might have inherited the sight, yet she wanted nothing to do with it. Nur was more like her mother and never saw any benefit in talking to the dead. Still, she hadn't been able to rid herself of the family legacy and somehow ended up becoming a historian. The past called to her.

These days people no longer believed in ghosts and goblins, which made it easier to ignore them. The living no longer had the time to seek out their dead loved ones and made sure they moved on to the next stage of their lives. People buried or burned were quickly forgotten by those still breathing.

Instead of answering him, she said, "What's your story?" If he were born in the castle, he might know its history better than anyone else. She could use him to verify some of the facts, at least.

"There isn't much I remember. All I know is that I once ruled these lands, then someone killed me, and I have been here since."

"Not much of a story," Nur said under her breath. She had moved further away from the hall and now faced a window, looking out at the horizon. Evening fast approached, and she felt like she had wasted yet another day. If only Mikal had taken an earlier flight. Without his help, she couldn't make a case to declare the castle a national treasure. Just imagining the rich history of this place made her smile.

The world moved away from the past on fast-forward, and people had the attention spans of fruit flies. Yet, if you ever stopped for long enough to take in the beauty past held, you would never be the same. It saddened her sometimes to know how much of Tibet's history went unrecorded. That's why this place interested her so much.

He must have felt embarrassed by her remark, which she didn't mean as an offense, because he added, "I remember my name. It's Gesar."

That got her attention, and she looked at him once again. "Your name is Gesar, and you were a king once? That's what you said?" she said, seeking confirmation.

"Yes, I am Gesar Lhobo Zhadui."

Nur was speechless. If he told the truth, the pride in his voice was well-deserved. But how could he be telling the truth? King Gesar was nothing but a myth. Although the Tibetans and Mongolians would say otherwise, the only thing history told about him came from oral stories bards had sung in these regions for as long as anyone could remember.

She wasn't well-versed in the epic of Gesar of Ling, but as far as she knew, there was nothing about his death. The man claimed he had come out of ancient folklore. Before she got over-excited, Nur recalled a conversation with her grandmother. Ghosts that had roamed the earth for a century, or more, might be unreliable. They could forget their origin and sometimes even develop false memories. She couldn't believe him unless he remembered the exact circumstances of his death and who killed him.

Ghosts might be wrong about many things from their past life, but they could never mistake the circumstances of their death. And in his case, it was a violent death, which meant if he remembered his murderer, it would be the truth.

TRUTH WITHIN THE LIES

Whether his memories were real or fake, didn't matter to Nur. The man fascinated her, and she wanted to know more about him. Even if he could tell little about his life, he must remember things while he was a ghost. A century's worth of knowledge and observation meant talking to him would be fun.

It was the first time she had encountered a ghost older than her. Most people would move on to the afterlife by their tenth death anniversary, making it yet another thing about him that grabbed her attention.

"Okay, I have decided," she declared, making a vague gesture with her hands. "I'll help you remember your past, and if you are who you say you are, then you'll help me write history that has remained unwritten until now." After delivering her grand statement, she waited for his excited response. None came.

The man, who had been bewildered until

then, was now stoic. He was no less handsome, though. "So?"

But before he could say anything, the guard approached her and said, "Miss, excuse me." He must have seen her talking and might now be thinking her insane. "You have to leave the grounds. It's getting dark, and I'm sorry, but no one is allowed here after the dark." He fidgeted and looked around superstitiously as if a ghost or a goblin would suddenly reach out to him.

Nur sighed. She couldn't keep talking to Gesar in the presence of the guard. He was the same one she had met the last time she visited the castle. As annoyed as she was by the interruption, she knew he was right. The castle grounds weren't well-lit, and the place wasn't safe for anyone roaming about in the dark. Unless, of course, you were a ghost.

Gesar remained quiet. He could have said something. It wasn't like the guard could hear him, but he said nothing. With another regretful sigh, Nur followed the guard out of the castle gates and down the dirt road. The watch tower was about a ten-minute walk from the castle, and the parking lot was further down the road. By the time she reached her car, it was already dark, but that didn't matter to her. She was no novice when it came to driving down winding mountain roads.

She might be a foreigner in Tibet, but her hometown was a valley much like this one—a beautiful place tucked away between the mountains of the Himalayan range. Well, if you went further down the history-road and flipped through the pages of the past, you would know it was once a part of the great Tibetan empire. The thought reminded her that not everyone appreciated the intricate webs past wove around the present.

Yet, she was disappointed Gesar's lack of interest in receiving her help. Perhaps, he didn't trust her enough to let her see into his memories. After all, he wasn't the one who sought out assistance from her. He might not even be interested in uncovering the truth behind his death. She couldn't begin to understand the kind of trauma recalling your death must leave behind.

As a seer, she assumed all ghosts wanted to know the lives they lived and the circumstances leading to their demise. At least, that was what her training—the little that she had from her grandmother—told her. He might be different, though. Someone not willing or ready to unravel the traumatic events of his life or death.

She tried to shake away these thoughts to no avail. Without realizing it, she ended up in her favorite place, a library. It was the first place she had visited as soon as she arrived in Tibet. Whenever troubling thoughts assaulted her, she would find refuge among books. Nothing could soothe her ruffled feathers like the musty smell of old books. Something was intoxicating in the knowledge that all the information held between their pages could be hers. All she had to do was pick them up, one by one, and read.

Later that night, she dreamed of a castle and a time long ago. The things that were somehow the most precious to her even though she had never experienced them. She walked down the corridors, followed by the court ladies, and laughed at the silliest things. Castle guards bowed down to her in respect, and she marveled at the influence she wielded. And she knew nothing was out of her reach. In that place and in that time, she held all the power.

△△△

A knock on the door woke her up. Groggily, Nur got out of bed to answer. Mikal stood there, smiling. She groaned and gestured for him to come in. "Isn't it too early to wake me up? I'm technically vacationing, you know."

"You could have fooled me by the number of phone calls I have been receiving daily," he said, laughing. "And it's not early at all. It's ten in the morning. Honestly, the lack of an early morning call to nag me about work worried me."

"If you're trying to be funny, don't." Without another word, she went to the washroom to freshen up. Mikal would wait in her room or go down to the lobby. Either way, she didn't care. She was having trouble keeping her eyes open and needed to make herself presentable before she spoke to him.

"You know," he raised his voice so she could hear him from behind the closed door. "We can ditch work. It's a beautiful day. Let's not waste it and do some sightseeing."

Not getting a response, he continued, "You might have grown up in a place like this, but I haven't been to a place as picturesque as the Himalayas. Let me be a tourist for one day. What do you think?"

That's when she came out of the washroom, feeling more like a human, and replied, "Normally, I would say no. But for some reason, I don't want to work today. My mind is still lost in my dream." A wistfulness gripped her senses and she barely refrained from sighing deeply.

By Mikal's shocked expression, she knew he hadn't expected her to agree. She sighed, not caring what he might think. From the moment she had opened her eyes, she had felt like a stranger in her own body.

"Nur, are you okay?"

"I'm fine. I just need a break and maybe a day of sightseeing and leisurely walks will revive my sanity." She smiled. "Besides, you have a point. How can I deprive you the pleasure of being a tourist?"

At the lightheartedness of her tone, Mikal returned her smile and seemed to breathe easier. "Perfect, let's meet downstairs in ten minutes."

Once he left, her thoughts returned to the dream and she had to force herself to come back to reality.

She had always enjoyed Mikal's company, who was a dear friend before a colleague. A day spent with him sounded divine, and seeing the place from his eyes might give her a new perspective. Something she needed because she might not have visited this side of Tibet before, but she was familiar with the region. Growing up in Baltyul, which literally meant 'Little Tibet,' natural beauty wasn't unknown to her. Nor was the culture wholly unfamiliar. The way things were, she might need a fresh set of unbiased eyes more than she realized.

BE STILL MY DEAD HEART

Gesar always thought he would die on a battlefield, even hoped it would be so. Because what better way to go than to breathe his last at the end of a sword like a true warrior? But he never considered he would only get half of his wish by dying at the hand of a coward who would plunge a sword into the heart of an unarmed man.

The betrayal wasn't the only thing keeping him tethered to earth. A sense of wrongness was partly to be blamed. He could never have imagined that when the time came, after all the battles he fought, death would come at the hands of a loved one—a close friend or perhaps family. If only he could remember the details about his life and death. Maybe he would find some solace within the layers of truth. Instead all he had was a vague memory and feelings that wouldn't let him rest in peace.

He wasn't a lucky man. When the woman offered to help him remember, it took him aback. If such a thing was possible, should he do it? Or was ignorance better? If his killer was someone close to him, did he want to learn the truth? The question plagued his next few days and nights, adding to his restlessness.

The answer should have been easy, but it wasn't. As much as his soul desired tranquility, things could still get worse. After all, he couldn't go back in time to right the wrong done to him. No matter how much he wanted revenge, it wouldn't be possible for him to execute it. What would he do? Everyone he knew was long gone.

"It's beautiful, isn't it?"

A soft voice, too close for his liking, startled Gesar. He was so deep in his thoughts that the woman snuck up on him without detection.

She now stood at his side and, following his gaze, looked at the mountain peaks. It was mid-afternoon. The sun shone brightly over the mountain tops, soaking the snow-covered peaks in an ethereal glow.

"It is," he said, no longer staring at the far horizon, but instead looking at her profile. "You came back."

It wasn't a question, so she didn't reply. "You never answered me. Do you want me to help you remember the past?" She didn't look at him and kept staring out the window. "Seers can help spirits and ghosts. I might not be as good as my grandmother, and a little out of practice, but I'm sure it's like riding a bicycle."

He didn't understand what she meant by that. Gesar knew what a bicycle was. One of the young princes, back in the nineteenth century, was rather fond of the thing. But he had never ridden it and couldn't understand what riding a bicycle would be like.

She looked at him then and smiled at his confused expression. "Never mind bicycles. What do you think about my offer?" she said, raising her eyebrows.

Instead of a straight answer, he said, "You never told me your name." He couldn't be sure why that was important, but he thought knowing her better might help him decide. The woman had caused ripples in his somewhat-peaceful existence, and he needed to understand why.

"Didn't I introduce myself? Oh, how rude of me," she said with a little exaggeration. "My name is Nur Bakht, and I'm a historian. I might know a few things about your life." She shrugged, trying to appear nonchalant.

He doubted that. After all, what could anyone know anything about someone from the prehistoric era? But he didn't point that out. "You're not from around here, though you speak the language well."

"I know almost all dialects of Tibetan. Languages are another one of my passions. You can't know the history of the people unless you know their language."

A sadness took hold of his heart. Something danced at the corners of his mind—a memory he couldn't reach. It waited there as if challenging him to grasp it in his hands. When he spoke, the words weren't his. "We only learned two things; how to fight and how to keep ourselves warm. Reading and learning were luxuries not afforded to us." He might not have intended to say that, but he knew the words were true.

Gesar watched as her smile faded, but she said nothing. After the silence stretched between them, she walked away. He followed, curious to see where she would go next. It seemed she didn't have any destination in mind. Aimlessly, she walked around and went outside to sit under a tree.

He didn't understand why his comment made her go silent like that. Had he said anything wrong?

"So, your offer," he said. Uncomfortable with the silence, he felt the urge to fill it. "How exactly does it work?"

"You're right," she said at last. But the words were unexpected. "About reading and learning. It's a luxury, and how sad we never consider it such."

The woman was strange if she still dwelled on that offhand comment. It wasn't a big deal. Time changed things. What's luxury today might become a necessity tomorrow. He considered how to change the topic once again, but there was no need to think as her striking eyes glazed over as if seeing right throw him.

Gesar crouched down next to her slumped form. She looked to be in some kind of trance. All humor left him as he watched her sitting still like a statue. Reaching out, he touched her shoulder, but his arm went right through her. He had forgotten ghosts couldn't touch the living. He could do nothing but watch over her, and wait for her to return from wherever her mind had traveled.

As the minutes passed, turning into hours, his fear rose. Nur entered his life like a ray of hope, and for the first time, he dared to think about the future. Now, she might never wake up, and the worst part was that he had an uncanny feeling about the whole situation. Like it was his fault somehow. Never had he ever felt this kind of fear before. As if something precious to him was about to be taken away, and he might never get it back.

"I told her to wait for me. How am I going to find her in this place," someone said from behind the tree line.

The voice was filled with annoyance with undertones of worry. Gesar watched as a young man appeared from behind the bushes, looking around as if searching for someone.

"Nur, where the hell are you?" He held a phone to his ear as he cursed loudly. "And she isn't even picking up the phone."

The guard appeared after him. "There!" He spotted Nur slumped form against the tree.

The two men rushed to her side, and when they couldn't bring her back from her stupor, they carried her away. Gesar followed them to the castle's gate, watching them leave and wondering what would happen now. All he could hope was for her to find the help she needed. He couldn't do anything for her, but maybe those men could.

THE KNOTS OF FATE

It was a beautiful day as she set out on her journey. The sun shone brightly, and the birds sang in the trees. Her open carriage made its way down the mountain path, rumbling and swaying gently on the uneven road. The horses neighed as it turned around a sharp bend. The sight that greeted Nur, took her breath away.

Atop a hill, in the distance, stood a magnificent castle. It's towers reached the sky, playing hide and seek with the clouds.

The place felt familiar to her heart, but she didn't remember it. All she knew was her undeniable need to see it up close and explore its secrets.

As her carriage drew nearer, she could see it was even more alluring than she thought. Her excitement grew with the anticipation of discovering something new and unexpected.

Then everything changed. Dark clouds gathered and enveloped the sun in their sinister embrace. The birds flew away and the sounds of nature faded with their retreat. The night seemed to sneak up on her uninvited, and the mountain path she knew like the back of her hand became treacherous, and her excitement turned into dread.

The castle was still there. Yet, where moments ago, she had felt as if it was brought to life from the pages of fairytales. Now, it seemed to have manifested from between the pages of history books —more real, somehow. The eeriness of it caused a chill to run down her spine.

Somewhere in the recesses of her mind, she knew she should go in the opposite direction of the imposing building, but she couldn't muster up enough will power to turn back the carriage, that moved forward on a steady pace. Horses trotting ahead as if they knew where they were taking her. As if under a spell, she drew closer to her doom. Unable to resist the pull or control the horses, she stayed on the path and tried to ignore the danger.

When she reached the castle, she realized it was more imposing up close; darker and foreboding, too. She still felt as if she had been there before, but she couldn't recall when or why.

The carriage entered the open castle gates, and she felt like she had been transported to another world. Just as before, when the day had turned into night within mere moments. Now, the night transformed into twilight—casting a musty hue over the place.

The horses stopped in front of a fountain in the courtyard and she stepped down. Her heart pounded in her chest, making her regret the decision of entering this place. But the decision was never hers and she knew that.

No one was around, and she was hyper-aware of her loneliness. Being alone in a strange place wasn't something a woman would find comfortable. She should turn back. It was obvious the castle had been abandoned long ago and was in ruins. She wouldn't find anything here. Not in the darkness that now enveloped the place.

The lights flickered in the castle windows, and she felt as if it had come alive. Though she still saw no one, she felt a sinister presence around her. As if someone else was there, who watched her every move. She could feel the eyes at the back of her neck.

Filled with terror, she entered through a tall wooden door. She could feel the eyes of unseen creatures upon her, but she bravely pressed on until she came to a large hall. Then, a sound boomed all around her. High-pitched and angry. *"It's all your fault!"* It accused and condemned her, *"You're to be blamed for this. It's all your fault!"*

△△△

"Nur, you need to take it more seriously,"

her grandmother admonished. "Dreams are the windows into the future. But they are of no help to you unless you know how to interpret them."

Of course, what she said made sense, but Nur wasn't in the mood to take anything seriously. "Mother thinks it's superstition."

"Your mother knows nothing." There was a hint of barely concealed anger beneath her words. "Besides, you're the one here to learn from me not her. I could never teach her anything."

She said the last part under her breath, but Nur heard it.

"Why does she hate it so much?" Nur gestured with her hands, trying to encompass everything, and shrugged, hoping her grandmother would know what she meant.

"She spent too much time in the West and has forgotten her roots. She might have given up on the ways of our ancestors, but she sent you here to learn. And that shows she doesn't hate it."

Her grandmother's voice might have been gentle, but Nur felt the barely concealed regret in the softness of her tone.

Sometimes, mothers and daughters had complicated relationships. Now that Nur considered it, she agreed with her grandmother. Though her mother never returned to Pakistan, she sent her to stay with her grandmother. That meant something.

Didn't it?

The sixteen-year-old Nur Bakht had come to the country of her birth for the first time after her parents left when she was still a child. In some ways, the place was exactly as she imagined, yet in others, it was surprising. That wasn't the most important thing, though. The real issue was the nightmares she had been having since the day she arrived there.

Her grandmother lived in Baltistan. A place as beautiful as it was shouldn't incite nightmares. Yet it did; to make matters worse, her grandmother took it *very* seriously.

"Dreams are not just dreams, Nur. They mean something, and you won't know what unless you learn to read between the lines." she appeared thoughtful before continuing, "In this latest dream of yours, you saw a castle that appeared inviting at first and then foreboding. Correct?"

Nur nodded, and her grandmother said, "The castle might be a real place or something else. However, I clearly see a choice here. Destiny is always a forked road, and whatever happens, will depend on the one you pick. It may lead you to something good, or it might cause you irrevocable pain. The decision will be yours, though. A day turning into night, and then twilight may hint at different timelines."

She sighed and stroked Nur's hair lovingly. "Ah, fate is a tricky mistress. She doesn't like to make things easy or simple."

△△△

Nur hadn't thought about the incident after that. Her grandmother had helped her block the nightmares, and that was it. She was never the one to dwell on personal things of the distant future or forgotten past, anyway. She hadn't even connected the dots when she saw the castle of Huangtong for the first time. Though the place had called to her, she hadn't understood why.

Now, sitting in a hospital bed and recalling her past, she wondered if it was the place she saw in the nightmares all those years ago. Whatever the case, she understood it was time to remember her grandmother's teachings and leave her mother's doubts behind. She would have to become the seer she was always meant to become, or she would never solve the mystery of king Gesar's death.

JOURNEY TO THE PAST

It was getting dark and bone-chilling cold. Traveling on the rocky, snow-covered uneven road and feeling like her insides rattled with every move forward, Zhumu inwardly cursed her mother-in-law. It would be Yelga Dzeiden's fault if her carriage toppled into the ravine or she froze to death. The carriage lurched again, coming to a stop, and this time, she cursed outwardly.

Jiacha Xiega knocked on the carriage window and said, "Are you all right, sister?" He rode on a horse beside the carriage.

"I'm fine. How much longer?"

"We're almost there. I'm sorry for the inconvenience, but I fear Yelga is the only one who can help Gesar now." The sadness in his words was palpable. "Something must be wrong, or he would have returned as soon as the war ended."

Jiacha was right, of course, but Zhumu didn't want to think about it. It had almost been twelve years without any news of Gesar. When she married him, she had an inkling of her future—their future. He wasn't just any king but a true leader, and all he wanted was to liberate his people. His entire purpose of existence was to guide his people into an era of enlightenment. For that to happen, they needed to be united and freed from war and hunger. He hated the tribal divisions and uncertainty that plagued their lands. His war wasn't to increase his power but to end all wars and save them from a reign of terror. And he had done it.

After a long battle, he defeated the demon king at last. King Toda was dead, and the people of *Deyu* lived in peace and harmony with the people of Ling. Yet, Zhumu waited and waited, but Gesar never returned. There had been no news of him. Meanwhile, his uncle coveted the throne, and she was the only one who stood in his way.

As the queen of Kingdom Ling, Zhumu tried to do her duty. She wasn't the one to cower. After all, there was a reason why people called her Sengcham Drugmo (Lion Sister Dragoness). She earned that title but now, she was getting impatient and tired of waiting. The internal threats to the kingdom aside, she missed her husband. It was about time he returned.

Jiacha Xiega's horse trotted alongside the carriage. He might be Gesar's half-brother, but he was no leader. As much as he wanted to side with Zhumu, he feared his uncle. Another reason why she needed Gesar. The only person who could keep his uncle's ambitions in check.

Finally, the carriage took a turn, and a lake came into view. The cold had half-frozen it. There was a small hut nearby, but as it turned out, that wasn't their destination. The carriage halted at the beach, and Jiacha jumped from his horse. He helped his sister-in-law to get off the carriage and guided her to the edge of the lake.

Noticing the dark hut and not seeing Yelga anywhere, Zhumu said, "Doesn't she know we are coming?"

Staring out at the icy still waters, Jiacha shrugged. "She knows, but time moves differently in the Naga realm. She will be here soon."

They didn't have to wait for long. Soon a thick mist hovered above the lake and surrounded them. The carriage and the horses hid from their sight. And from the mist, Yelga appeared like a phantom. She rose from the depths of the water and floated toward them. They watched, transfixed and in awe, as she came closer. Still, in her half-serpent form, she turned fully human only when she reached the beach.

"Mother," they said in unison and bowed their heads as was the custom.

"My, it has been years since I saw you last, dear daughter," Yelga said. The mist drifted away, and she engulfed Zhumu in a fierce hug. For Jiacha she had nothing but an icy glance. Not that anyone would blame her. After all, his mother was the catalyst that led to her and Gesar's banishment from the castle.

It was said the Nagas could hold a mean grudge, and from the steel in her mother-in-law's eyes, Zhumu believed that. The woman was gorgeous with her long, sleek black hair, almond-shaped eyes, and curvy figure of a goddess. *'But then,'* Zhumu thought, *'she was from a divine race and a Nagi princess, at that.'*

"So, tell me, child, what has been happening in the mortal realm and where is my son?" She looked over their shoulders, expecting Gesar to walk up to them any moment.

"Actually, that's what we wanted to discuss with you," Zhumu began nervously. She had heard tales of the Nagi's temper from Gesar and feared what the woman would do when she found out her son was missing. But they must tell her if they sought her help.

When Zhumu first met Gesar, it had come as a surprise to know he was half Naga. And though he couldn't shift to a snake form or breathe underwater, he had inherited his strength and steely resolve from his mother's race. The Nagas were a powerful, proud, and splendid semi-divine race of serpents. They protected the world but could also bring about natural disasters of great magnitude if provoked. Mostly, they were the bringers of prosperity and harmony to the world.

Perhaps, Gesar's need to do the same also originated from that side of the family.

Yelga listened to Zhumu patiently as the latter relayed Gesar's exploits, victories, and disappearance. In the end, she said, "Since the Naga realm reaches beyond ours, we hope you might be able to help us find him."

"That's not a problem. As long as there is water, my powers can reach it. I can tell you right now where he is. But how will you bring him back, that's the real question."

Long silence ensued the statement as Zhumu contemplated. Then, she asked, "Can't you help us?"

Where she had mastered the art of diplomacy and politics, Zhumu was no longer a fighter. She couldn't lead warriors, nor could she wield magic. If Yelga refused to intervene, she didn't know what she would do. The Nagi princess hadn't left her lake in two decades. Although, she might not have to do that since the Naga realm was an underground world with a network of streams that reached every corner of the earth.

"You know I can't leave the lake," Yelga confirmed what Zhumu had feared.

"No, I didn't know that," Zhumu said.

At the same time, Jiacha said, "Yes."

"It's true. It was one of the conditions of my banishment from Kingdom Ling and the only reason the late King spared Gesar's life. I'll have to spend the rest of my days on this piece of land and water."

"But Gesar is king now, and he can lift your banishment. Can't he?"

"Yes, he can. But he isn't here."

"I am, though. And I'm his queen," Zhumu declared. "I have been ruling in his place for the last twelve years. I can free you of this unjust condition."

This time Jiacha was the one who answered, "Sister, that's not how the magic of the realm works. King's word can't be undone except by him or the next king. Our father banished her to this valley, and when Gesar took his place, she refused to let him lift her banishment. Now, she will have to stay here." He paused and then looked at Yelga. "You can communicate with your people, though. Can't they help?"

The tension between Yelga and Jiacha was palpable. It was brave of him to stand in front of the Nagi princess and make suggestions. For a second, Zhumu feared her mother-in-law might curse him with her venom, but she didn't, and Zhumu admired her for that. Appreciating Yelga's regal posture, she thought her aloof attitude toward the son of her worst enemy wasn't only uncanny but beautiful.

"Let's first see where Gesar is and what's keeping him away from home and his wife."

MUCH IS LOST IN TIME

It had been so long since she saw her last vision that she had forgotten how much it took from her. And that's when she used to have normal visions—if there even was such a thing. But this one had been different. She wasn't just seeing the past, rather she was a part of it; she lived it.

"How long are you planning to stare at the bare wall?"

The question brought Nur's attention to Mikal. He sat on a chair beside her bed and gave her a concerned look. She didn't respond because she couldn't trust herself to speak.

"Do you know what happened?" he said.

Once again, she stayed silent. She knew she would have to answer at least some of his questions, but she didn't want to say anything. Her mind was still processing her visions of the past. No, not just the past but *her* past. The realization had struck her like lightning, yet there was no denying the fact.

"Nur, you're scaring me with your silence."

Unable to trust her voice, she raised a hand in the gesture of patience. With her eyes, she pleaded him to give her time. After that, he didn't say anything. He took her hand into his and joined her in staring at the walls. The silence wasn't awkward, though.

After what seemed like an eternity, Nur said, "How much do you know about the legend of king Gesar?"

Mikal looked at her as if she had lost her mind, but thankfully, he answered. "Not much. When I was a kid, we used to read stories about him. Isn't he a fictional character?"

"You know I spend most of my teenage in Baltyul." When he stared at her blankly, she added, "Baltistan."

"Right. Yes, I knew that."

"My grandmother used to tell me stories about him. Only she didn't call him Gesar. Instead, she used to call him Kesar, and according to her, he was a historical figure, a mighty king who did many remarkable deeds for his people. He battled demons, giants, and nine-headed ogres. She believed that whenever our world faced any danger from supernatural beings, king Kesar would be reborn to vanquish them to the other world. As a demigod, that's his destiny."

Mikal didn't interrupt as she continued, "Even though I have always been able to see ghosts and spirits, I never believed the stories. Isn't it strange?"

Hunched over with his elbows resting on his knees and his joined hands under his chin, he gave Nur an understanding glance. "I know what you mean. It's the same for me. Though you told me about being a seer, and I believe you. Still, there's doubt in my heart because I can't see ghosts. Honestly, I have never really *believed* believed you. If you know what I mean."

He sounded apologetic, but there was no reason because she did know. Ghosts might be real to her, but gods, goddesses, demons, and giants had always been a myth. To know that they actually existed, even if not in their realm but in realms connected to it, was just too much to take in. What did it mean for her and the ghost she unwittingly promised to help?

"What happened at the castle?"

To be fair, she didn't know how to answer him. One minute everything was fine as she talked to Gesar, and the next minute, she was back in her grandmother's house. And then, somehow, she was transported further back in the past. Though unusual, she could see her memories that she might have forgotten. Seers could get glimpses of their past and future when needed. She had been thinking about how best to help Gesar regain his memory, and that must have triggered hers. That much she understood.

Yet, how she was able to witness Zhumu and Jiacha's conversation with Gesar's mother, she couldn't understand. What's more, she had not just been an onlooker. She was Zhumu and saw everything from her point of view, but how? That had never happened before, and as much as she knew about her powers, it shouldn't have been possible unless it was all a dream while she was unconscious after her trance. But she knew it wasn't a dream.

Even if she were Zhumu's incarnation, it still wouldn't make sense for her to have these memories. Souls couldn't remember their past lives. Could they? Unfortunately, she didn't know much about it. Reincarnation wasn't something she believed in. It went against her faith, but how else to explain it. Her resemblance with Zhumu and her ability to witness Zhumu's life, what was it if not *that*.

"Nur?" Mikal's gentle voice made her feel guilty.

"I'm sorry, I don't understand everything. At first, I just had a vision of myself at my grandmother's place, and then, I—" she paused, unsure how to continue. "How long was I unconscious?" She changed the subject.

If Mikal noticed, he didn't point it out. "Two

days. Doctors weren't sure what was happening, so they just let you sleep. They said you would wake up when you were ready, and you did."

"Sorry for causing all the trouble." Finally, she gave him a genuine smile.

"Don't mention it."

She didn't tell Mikal about Gesar's ghost. It was strange, but she didn't want to talk about him. Her best friend might be privy to her family secret, yet that one she wanted to keep to herself.

"Nur, I will say something, and you aren't going to like this," he said while rubbing his forehead absentmindedly. "You should forget about the castle. I have looked into it, and there is no way our proposal will ever get approved."

That surprised Nur. Never had he ever considered giving up before they even started. She might only be a historian, but he was also an archeologist. "Why do you think that?" The question might be unnecessary, but she wanted to know how he would answer.

"People are wary of the place. Locals don't even go near it. I mean, didn't you notice how fearful the guards at the watch tower are? It's not because it's falling apart or anything. People believe it is haunted not by just ghosts but also demons."

Nur said nothing, but that was the lamest excuse she had ever heard. She didn't know why

Mikal wanted her to forget about the castle, but his reasoning was fake. It was she who possessed the power of seeing the unseen. Mikal didn't believe in the supernatural, and he was a scientist through and through. For him to give credence to local superstition meant there was more to it than he let on. He either knew something he didn't want her to know, or he was afraid. But why?

BACK TO THE BEGINNING

He contemplated only for a minute before he said, "Fine, maybe you're right. But do you know what every hero needs?"

There was a mischievous gleam in his eyes and a half-smile on his lips, Shampo's only clue that whatever Gawa was about to say wouldn't be anything good.

And he was proven right when Thopa Gawa made a grand gesture, spreading his arms wide, and doing a half-bow before saying, "A worthy adversary."

"What do you mean?" Shampo raised an eyebrow in query. In the realm of the gods, Gawa was well respected. His wisdom and heroism had always been admired and sometimes coveted. Yet, Shampo wasn't a big fan of his habit of overdramatizing everything. For Gawa, the world was literally a stage, and everyone else was an actor. If only he would take his job more seriously instead of his flair for the dramatic.

"I mean that if I am to be reborn on earth to help humans—yet again, I might add—I need helpful companions and a villain who will bring out the best in me. Heroes aren't made in a day or two, you know."

Shampo sighed in defeat. In truth, he already had a plan in motion to help Gawa's reincarnation and his journey to bring the world into an era of enlightenment. But he wanted it to happen on his terms. "It has already been decided. You will need guidance from the Naga realm and fight demons to become the hero you are meant to be. And then the humans will follow you into the light," he concluded with a shrug.

Apart from eight creator gods and goddesses, no one had the authority or the power to interfere in the human realm. That didn't mean they were unaware of the troubles of the humans, nor were they indifferent. That was why every once in a while, a demigod or goddess was chosen to be reborn as a human and live a life of a hero. Their only purpose would be to gain strength and enough followers to bring humans out of the darkness that plagued their hearts and souls.

Thopa Gawa had done it before, many times in fact. His success rate meant that now, it was his only job. After every few centuries, when the world was shrouded in despair and humanity was at its worst, he would go to earth and bring much-needed hope back into the hearts of humans. Looking at the young demigod, Shampo wasn't sure anymore. Gawa was getting arrogant and that didn't bode well for the mission. What if something went wrong?

"I suspected that much, but I have a specific demon in mind. Let Zanpu be the one to play my adversary."

"You are joking, surely." Shampo couldn't believe his ears. Things were far worse than he anticipated if Gawa thought releasing Zanpu from the underworld was a good idea. Thopa Gawa was no fool, though. He was an enlightened being who could reincarnate at will. The world needed him more than it ever did before, and in the hour of need, he was demanding to free Zanpu. Not only that but to allow him to be reborn alongside Gawa. Preposterous! That's what it was. "It took us the better part of three centuries to defeat him and send his soul to the mountain of damned. How can you so nonchalantly ask for his release?"

"I know what I'm asking for and have my reasons."

The finality of his tone gave the creator god a pause. He stared at Gawa with a penetrating look and weighed their options. Should he agree or ask for a second opinion before doing something that drastic?

DEAD HEARTS DON'T BEAT

Gesar needed a distraction, but what? Nur hadn't returned since that fateful day, and he worried something might have happened to her. To make matters worse, he couldn't stop thinking about her. She was all he had thought about since the day he met her. Between her and the queen of his memories, he didn't know whom he loved and missed more. He sighed deeply and walked around aimlessly--not knowing what to do or how to put himself out of this misery.

"Hiss...sss."

The sound startled him, and he stopped in his tracks. A snake uncoiled from where it sat under a tree and slithered toward him. Gesar didn't move. It wasn't that he was scared of the thing--after all, what could a snake do to a ghost--rather, it fascinated him. Its movements were measured, and its eyes were trained on him. As if it had been lying in wait.

"Found you."

For a second, Gesar couldn't believe his ears. The snake hissed, but he understood the words. *Found you*. What could that mean? Considering his next move, he stared blankly, but the snake didn't give him time to react, say or do anything. It vanished behind the bushes, leaving him wondering if it was his imagination or did it talk. He thought about following it, but another voice stopped him.

"Gesar."

His name on her lips inspired him. He hadn't realized how worried he had been until he saw Nur's smiling face. "You are back."

"Of course I am. Didn't I say I'll help you?" She walked up to him and stretched to look over his shoulder. "What were you staring at?"

"Nothing, it was just a snake. It's gone now," he added quickly to reassure her.

"Right, I'm not afraid of the snakes. In case you are wondering."

"No, the thought didn't occur to me." He smiled then, not a polite one he had given her before, but a full, happy smile that reached his eyes and brightened them. He realized with a start that he *was* happy to see her. In all the time since he woke up dead, he hadn't been happy for even a single moment. He should say something before he made a fool of himself by confessing his undying love to the woman or some such nonsense. Clearing his throat, he said, "What happened to you the other day?" That seemed like a safe topic to talk about.

Nur looked away then and seemed to be considering her words carefully. "I had a vision," she said at last after the silence between them stretched, bordering on uncomfortable. "It was about you. But also, about me." She went quiet again. Folding her hands behind her, she strolled down the garden path.

Gesar said nothing and followed her. It looked like she was struggling with words. Perhaps, she didn't want to tell him about the vision. But he couldn't think why. All kinds of horrible scenarios came to his mind. Did something bad happen in her vision?

It might be because he hadn't spoken to anyone in centuries. Or he might have always been a patient man, but he didn't prompt her to elaborate. She would tell him in her own time. Walking around in circles, she seemed to be collecting her thoughts. Finally, she stopped and looked directly at him.

Taking a deep breath, she said, "You were gone."

"Huh?" Of all the things he had imagined her saying, that definitely wasn't one of them. "Gone where? When?"

She laughed and looked sheepish. "I'm a historian. You would think I knew better than to start a story in the middle." She looked around as if trying to find an excellent spot to sit.

Thinking of the snake, Gesar stopped her with a gesture and pointed toward the stairs that led to a pavilion. "Maybe we should sit there." He could tell she was troubled by something, but that didn't dampen his mood. Just seeing her and being able to talk to her was exhilarating. She was there with him. And somehow he felt as if it was all he needed. He couldn't fully comprehend let alone put his feelings into words but he wanted to make her comfortable. When she sat down on a stair, he followed suit.

"Okay, so," she began. "As I told you, I'm a seer. I can see ghosts, talk to them, and help them remember their past. But I can also see into my own past and sometimes, even future." She looked at him as if making sure he was following her. So, he nodded, and she continued, "Last time when I was here, I went into a trance. Unexpected, but it wasn't unusual. I saw my past. Something I had forgotten; this castle in my dreams, to be precise."

"You dreamed of this place?"

"Yes, that's right, but that's not important."

"It's not?"

"No, I don't think so. I had those dreams when I was a teenager. They might be a glimpse of my future, which has already happened, now that I'm here. I have found this place. So, that part of the vision is no longer important. It's the next part that's been bothering me."

"Okay," he said as if telling her to go on.

"I'm a queen in this vision. And I'm talking to a Nagi princess."

Now, she had lost him completely. He had no idea what she was saying or trying to say. Then, the word "queen" registered, and he wondered, even hoped, if his suspicion was true because he, too, had dreamed about a queen, *his* queen. The woman he loved more than anyone else in the world, the same woman who fell out of love and condemned his soul.

"I think I'm the reincarnation of your wife."

Her tone was matter-of-fact, but the words rocked his world yet again. It shook him to his core. No wonder the woman felt so familiar. No wonder his dead heart longed for her--to be with her. No wonder he was dreaming once again. And no wonder he fell in love with her at first sight. His soul recognized hers even if his mind hadn't connected the dots. Nur's appearance started ripples in his somewhat stagnant life, and for a good reason.

As soon as the ray of hope bloomed in his heart, the cloud of doubts engulfed it. He was dead. No matter what their past was or how much he loved the woman in front of him. The bottom line remained that he died while she lived. God gave her rebirth while his soul was still tethered to earth, unable to move on to the next stage of the afterlife.

THE CRUEL LIES

They were no longer alone. Gesar could feel a presence even though he couldn't see who it was. There was someone else in the castle watching them without revealing himself. He racked his head, trying to remember if any other creature roamed the place, but nothing came to mind.

Nur must have noticed his alertness because she said, "What is it?"

He considered lying to spare her the worry, but lies never served any purpose. And he never lied. "Someone is watching us." His eyes roamed in all four directions, trying to pinpoint the source of his discomfort.

She also looked around but saw no one. "Are you sure? I don't see another ghost."

"It's not a ghost." Before he said anything else, a man came into his line of vision. He squinted to make out his profile and realized it was the same person who had come looking for Nur the other day.

"Oh, it's just Mikal," she whispered to him. And much loudly, she said, "What are you doing here?"

"What do you think? I'm trying to make sure nothing else happens to you." His tone was annoyed. "Why did you leave without a word, Nur?"

"I didn't know I needed your permission."

"Please, don't twist my words. You were in the hospital, and after recovering first thing you do is, come back here." He looked frustrated. "Why are you obsessing over this place? It's not the first historical castle you have ever come across, nor would it be the last." He shook his head and took a deep breath. The guy was trying to understand her actions and failing.

"He must not know about me," Gesar said aloud, but Nur ignored him and kept her eyes on Mikal.

"I don't know why you are overreacting. I told you this place is important..."

He cut her off. "But why? That's what I don't understand."

The storm brewing in Nur's eyes scared Gesar. This Mikal guy didn't seem to understand he treaded on thin ice. There was something between those two that Gesar couldn't understand. He would have thought them best friends, but Nur wasn't honest with him if she kept Gesar's existence a secret. Or

Mikal didn't know anything about her being a seer. Though why she would hide something like that wasn't understandable. The world was different, and it was possible people didn't look upon such things favorably. As curious as he was, he thought it better to refrain from interfering. After all, he didn't know Mikal or the relationship those two shared. Maybe they weren't friends at all.

There was silence as Mikal and Nur stared at each other without saying anything. Meanwhile, Gesar looked at the two, interested to see what would happen next. Before anyone could say anything, the snake reappeared. No one saw it approach, but it positioned itself between Nur and Mikal. The snake hissed loudly and startled them all.

"What?" Mikal and Gesar said at the same time, while Nur just blinked at it rapidly.

This time when Gesar looked at Mikal, he saw him differently. He was sure the other man couldn't see him. But he had understood what the snake said. Gesar was certain of that.

And Nur noticed it too because she now looked at Mikal curiously. "Did you just talk to a snake?"

"No, don't be absurd." He looked away from her, ignoring the snake and trying not to look guilty.

The snake didn't repeat itself and slithered away as if it couldn't care less about their quarrel. Funny, Gesar could swear it just told him to go to the pond on the other side of the garden.

"Is there a pond on the other side?" Mikal asked Nur, confirming Gesar's suspicion. He did understand the snake, but since he couldn't see ghosts, he probably thought the snake was talking to him. But why would he think that instead of just ignoring the creature? Gesar was sure of one thing, though. There was more to this guy than met the eye.

"Yes, there is. Why do you ask?"

"No reason. Maybe I should look around now that I'm here." This time Mikal's tone was completely different. He sounded interested in the place.

Gesar didn't like his change in attitude. The guy must be up to something. Hoping she wouldn't question him and do as he asked, he said to Nur, "Don't take him to the pond. In fact, it's better if you two leave."

Thankfully, she took the hint because she also changed her tone and said, "You know what, you were right. What was I thinking? I don't even feel that well. Maybe we should go." She stood up and walked away.

As expected, Mikal followed her. Gesar couldn't hear what he said in response, but he didn't care. His attention was now on the pond and the mysterious snake who could talk. Or rather, he could understand it.

THE NAGI PRINCESS

"Took you long enough," the snake hissed when it saw Gesar approach the pond. "Follow me."

Instead of following the snake, Gesar halted and said, "How can I understand you?" He was struggling to wrap his mind around the fact that he could talk to snakes. It was yet another one of those things that had never happened before. Did meeting Nur change him somehow? But why? The questions were beginning to make him more restless than he had ever been before.

"Of course, you can. Your highness is half-Naga."

With those words, a memory of his mother resurfaced, and Gesar gasped. Understanding dawned on him as he stared out at the pond. Any substantial body of water was a gateway to the Naga realm. He knew that because he had witnessed his mother emerging from within the depths of a lake. That's why the snake wanted to bring him here. "I can't breathe underwater," he said regretfully.

"You're already dead," the snake hissed.

"Yes, well." Was the snake being sarcastic? "Are you saying I can enter the Naga realm now that I'm a ghost?"

Though the snake said nothing, Gesar heard it loud and clear. "Duh!"

As a kid, Gesar often asked his mother to bring him to the Naga palace with her, but he was more human than Naga. Visiting the Naga realm or meeting his maternal side of the family wasn't in the cards for him. Or so he believed, but now he no longer needed to breathe.

It might not trigger his curse because even if he entered the Naga realm under the pond, he would technically still be in the castle. Before then, he never considered the possibility because he had forgotten his past and his Naga heritage. Now that he remembered his mother, things looked promising. She might help him remember more of his past and even help him with his current predicament.

"Come on, what are you waiting for?" The snake vanished in the water, leaving Gesar with no other choice but to follow.

The underwater world was nothing like he expected. He imagined a landscape full of vibrant and varied life forms, but it was much more peaceful and tranquil. Gesar marveled at the color palette created as the sunlight filtered through the water. He swam behind the snake and went further down into the pond. The deeper they went, the darker it got until they reached the bottom. Then, everything brightened once again.

The depths captivated him. He watched in fascination as water dragons swam around him before continuing on their way. Vibrant colors, exotic creatures with tentacles, others with scales, and still more that were a combination of the two, and majestic scenery assaulted his senses. The realm of the Nagas was far more magical than he anticipated. They swam past a shipwreck, and a walled city came into view, whose gates were guarded by the giant sea serpents.

From where they hovered in the water, Gesar couldn't see the top of the city walls and wondered if they could swim over them. There was no need, though. The snake that accompanied him stopped near the guards and said something. The next thing Gesar knew, gates swung open as if by magic, and they entered the underwater city. Thus far, they had been swimming. Now, on their own accord, his feet touched the solid ground, and he walked on. Most people were in their snake form, but some preferred half-human and half-serpent personas. The only one in complete human form was a woman he recognized as soon as his eyes found her.

Yelga, his mother--the Nagi princess, must

have been waiting for them. As soon as she saw them coming, she rushed forward and engulfed him in a tight hug. "My son, how many centuries have I waited to see you again? How have I searched for you? I never imagined finding you in such a way. A ghost?" Her voice clogged with tears as she buried her face into his chest.

"Mother." Gesar hugged her back. Her warmth surrounded his dead heart and a weight lifted from his soul. His mother was alive and well. She was here, and he could touch her. He tried hard not to burst into tears himself. He hadn't felt the touch of another living being in what seemed like an eternity.

His father banished the two of them when he was a mere boy. At the time, he was too young to understand what was happening, but later, he found out about the treachery of his father's second wife. The woman was vile and remained so until the very end. Even after his father died, she did everything she could to thwart his claim to the throne. He was the firstborn, and it was not only his birthright but also his destiny to lead the people of Kingdom Ling. Thankfully, his stepbrothers were nothing like their mother and welcomed him with open arms.

For a long time, though, it had just been him and his mother. They lived in exile, far from the castle, and fended for themselves. The bond he shared with her was unbreakable. There was no one else he loved more. How he could have forgotten this was a mystery to him. But his memories of her were rushing back with a vengeance.

"Let me look at you." She detached herself from his embrace and drew back to stare at his face. Once she had her fill, she took his hand into hers and led her through the city.

In the distance, he could see a beautiful marble palace surrounded by glowing crystal gardens. Nagas were friendly and welcoming people. Everyone they met on their way to the palace greeted them with a respectful bow and a smile.

It was hard to believe that such a world existed below theirs. In every building and every structure, he could feel the history and culture that had existed for thousands of years.

As it turned out, his mother was no longer the princess. She was the queen, ruling over the entire realm and trying to maintain the balance between worlds. Taking the throne meant she could no longer leave the realm even for a little while. The thought saddened Gesar, and he wondered if she missed their home by the lake. That small cottage had been their sanctuary for years.

They walked toward the palace, which grew bigger as they came nearer. From above, it had been a small pond, but below it, the vastness of the place was immeasurable.

"Are we still under the castle?" he said, fearful of finding himself back in the dungeons.

"My dear son, you are in another realm. It has nothing to do with the human world, and the laws of your realm don't matter here. You are under my protection, and here my magic is stronger than any on earth."

Her words reassured him, and he sighed in relief. Then a thought occurred to him, and he said, "You have been looking for me? But I thought I was dead."

He couldn't be sure about his life, but nothing in death had made sense. This might be the time he found out the truth about a few things, at least.

His mother sighed. "It's a long story. Where do I begin?"

"Beginning is usually a good place to start." He smiled.

THE MYSTERY IN MAYHEM

Nur let Mikal escort her back to the hotel. She wasn't sure what had happened, but she could tell Gesar wanted them to leave as soon as possible.

Mikal wasn't a stranger to her. She had known him for years, and they had been best friends for almost half of that time. Yet, there was something unfamiliar about the way he was treating her.

His trying to dissuade her from visiting the castle ruins was only one of the things grating on her nerves. And what had bothered her the most was that his reaction had been different when she had talked to him over the phone. She wondered what changed and why was he now adamant she should leave Tibet and forget about the castle.

"Are you feeling better?" Mikal said.

Concern laced his tone, and worry lines etched his face, reminding her of the friend he was.

Why, then, could she not feel the sincerity in his words?

"No, not really." Se lied and touched her forehead as if feeling dizzy. "I think I'm going to call it a day. Maybe tomorrow I'll feel better."

"Yes, maybe."

The look he gave her showed how little he believed her. But then, she had never been a good liar.

"You don't need to babysit me, really," she said as he tried to follow her into the room. "I'm just going to rest for a while." She gave him what she hoped was a tired smile.

He didn't say anything else and left. Nur could tell there was something else on his mind. And she had a gut feeling he would return to the castle. Her only hope was that Gesar already did whatever it was he wanted to do.

She would go there tomorrow and ask him what it was. Until then, she might as well take this opportunity and catch up on much-needed sleep because she sure was exhausted.

∆∆∆

"That makes no sense. Why would he still be there?" It was the hundredth time Zhumu had asked the question. Yet, neither her mother-in-law nor her brother-in-law had any satisfactory answer.

"Sister," Jiacha said, carefully picking his words, "maybe there is something we don't know. There's no reason to jump to the wrong conclusion. Gesar loves you. Everyone knows that."

Zhumu's eyes filled with tears, and she closed them as if willing them away. She considered herself a strong woman and didn't like being emotional in front of others.

Well aware of her husband's duties, she had never complained once. No matter how often he was away from home, she had remained steadfast in her belief that the world needed him more than she did. This time though, she couldn't help but feel betrayed—cheated.

"Daughter, as much as it pains me to admit it, Jiacha is right," Yelga said.

The pity in the older woman's eyes broke Zhumu's heart more than the fact that Gesar was choosing not to return.

Keeping her voice soft, Yelga continued, "We only know he is staying at Deyu, but we don't know why. It might not be because of Maisa, as you fear. Maybe there is some other threat we are yet unaware of."

The words made sense, but Zhumu's heart refused to accept them. "I wish to go to Deyu myself. The demon king is dead, and Maisa has taken over the throne. There is no reason for Gesar to be there. *With that woman.*" She hated how jealous she felt, but Maisa was once meant to be Gesar's concubine. Why else would he stay in *her* palace if not for some lingering feelings?

"I advise against it," Yelga tusked. "You must remain in your Kingdom, or else Gesar's uncle might start his campaign to take over the throne."

"The courtiers are becoming restless as they, too, wait for their king to return. Maybe I should go to Deyu and find out what's happening there," Jiacha added.

"For once, I agree with my stepson," Yelga said. "He can leave at once and bring his brother home."

At Yelga's suggestion, Zhumu saw relief in Jiacha's eyes. She understood their fears. They wanted to protect Ling, but she wanted to protect her heart. Still, how could she act selfishly when Gesar had sacrificed everything for his people and his country?

She was a mere girl of sixteen when she met Gesar. He was visiting Hor and stayed at their palace. At the time, she didn't know him well and had only heard of his heroic deeds through palace gossip. Back then, she thought people exaggerated, but meeting him changed her mind. He was everything they said and more. Her heart had belonged to him since the day she set her eyes on him.

At the age of eighteen, Gesar wasn't interested in finding a wife. His heart was at his next battlefield. He was always thinking of the next monster to slay. It had taken Zhumu a while to convince him of her devotion and undying love. But even then, he hadn't made any proclamation of love. Marrying Hor's princess had made political sense, and that's all their marriage was to him.

Soon, it all changed and their first few years together were pure bliss. A half-smile appeared on Zhumu's face as she reminisced about their past. Though he never claimed to love her, he sent Maisa away as soon as they returned to Ling.

At the time, it hadn't mattered but in hindsight, sending half-demoness back to Deyu might have been the wrong move. The partying was amicable, or so it had seemed, but there hadn't been a just cause for it. It was no surprise that the demon king rebelled against them. The rebellion came years later and maybe Maisa had nothing to do with it or with Gesar's current absence. Yet, her heart said otherwise.

As if knowing what Zhumu was thinking, Yelga said, "Maisa might have expected to become Gesar's concubine once, but it was before he even met you. Besides, it wasn't a love match. And I assure you, the demon king never cared for his daughter enough to wage a because of her. His reasoning was nothing but the seed of evil in his heart."

"I know." Zhumu sighed deeply. "You're right, and it has already been years since Maisa left Ling."

It had been twenty years, to be precise. But what could she do when her heart said there was something wrong and Gesar's stay in Deyu wasn't an innocent coincidence?

Turning to Jiacha, she said, "Then you will go, brother, and bring him home?"

He took her hands in his and promised to bring Gesar back no matter what. Only then, Zhumu could breathe easily. She knew she could trust Jiacha's promise because he loved his half-brother. And also, the Nagi princess was their witness and would hold him accountable. She only hoped he wouldn't take long. Twelve years of separation had already been more torture than her heart could endure.

△△△

Nur opened her eyes and stared at the ceiling. The emotional turmoil brought on by the dream had her soul in its grasp. She felt tears streaming down her cheeks. Sending Jiacha to bring Gesar back had been the worst mistake of her life—the one she would regret forever.

THE UNTOLD TALE

"It started in the heavens, as these things mostly do. Gods pretend they don't interfere in human lives and keep the promise of free will, but it's far from the truth. They are always playing games with humans. Tying the threads of fate when they want and moving humans across the board like chess pieces." Yelga took a deep breath. The anger she felt toward the gods and goddesses of the mountains ran so deep she couldn't have stopped her tirade even if she wanted.

"You are my son," she said, pressing Gesar's face between her hands. Her gaze was filled with longing and regret. "But also, the reincarnation of the demi-god Thopa Gawa. You came to earth with a predestined mission.

"The gods sent a plague to Naga's realm and pretended to cure it. In return, they demanded that I spend one year on earth. My father had no choice but to comply. No one knew the game gods were playing. I thought I'd explore the earth for a year and then return to the Naga realm."

As she paused to collect her thoughts, Gesar watched her closely. He might have remembered his mother and a few cherished moments with Zhumu, but most of his memories were still missing. He knew now how proud he had always been of his Naga heritage, but to think gods manipulated his parents for him to reincarnate as half-Naga turned his stomach in disgust. His mother was right when she said they were pawns in whatever game the gods played.

"You were going to defeat the demon king, thus uniting the lands and bringing humans into an era of enlightenment. Things didn't go as planned, as we know. I am unsure exactly why or how, but Maisa betrayed and cursed you. You lost your memories and stayed with her in Deyu after winning the war against her father."

A tear rolled down her cheek as if recalling the past was physically painful for her.

Gesar tried to remember who Maisa was, but he couldn't. The name didn't bring back any memories or feelings. Whoever she was, she must not have been important to him.

The most important things was to know what happened and how he died. So, he urged his mother to continue, and she did.

"For twelve years, no one in Ling knew what happened to you. Once the news of the demon king's demise reached your castle, Zhumu asked me to discover the truth. She feared the worst, and she wasn't wrong. But we made a mistake when we sent Jiacha to find you instead of Zhumu." This time his mother's gaze was apologetic.

Gesar knew the name Jiacha. It was someone he had once considered a friend. Maybe even a brother. Who was it? He tried to remember, and a picture formed in his mind, but the face that appeared in his head was of Mikal, Nur's friend. He thought it odd, but assumed his brain was playing tricks since he couldn't remember the face to go with the name.

"Who was Jiacha?" he asked. Until then, he had been listening to her mother's tale without interrupting her, but he was becoming impatient.

"Jiacha was your half-brother. He loved you, but he wasn't a brave man. His cowardice cost you your life, and the world lost the hero it needed the most. Instead of finding the antidote for the curse Maisa had cast, he returned and told Zhumu you were staying in Deyu willingly, and she should move on with her life."

"What?" he gasped. "Why would he do that?"

The thought of such a lie made his heart ache. Zhumu must have hated him. She must have felt betrayed, and the hurt caused by his half-brother's lie must have been impossible for her to forget or forgive.

"He was scared of Maisa, but the lie was cruel,

and what happened next was something none of us could have anticipated."

Ah, but Gesar knew Zhumu. He could imagine what must have happened next. If Jiacha thought she would accept his betrayal and move on with her life, he was mistaken. His queen wouldn't have stopped until she faced Gesar and demanded an explanation. He could picture it clearly. The Dragon Sister Lioness was no weakling. His mother's next words proved him right.

"No matter how much Jiacha tried to stop her, Zhumu picked up the sword and led the army to Deyu herself. Maisa couldn't let you meet with her because she feared the bond you shared would break the curse. Instead, she met Zhumu's army with one of her own. They both died on the battlefield."

Gesar had often wondered about his past and the people in it. Over the centuries, he had imagined many scenarios and concocted various stories about his life. Yet, not even in his wildest dreams had he considered such an ending. He was the warrior cursed to forget the woman he had loved. While that woman had fought on his behalf and died the death, he should have faced himself.

One thought lingered and he asked the most dreaded question of all, "What happened to me?"

"To be honest, no one knows. Once the dust settled, you were nowhere to be found. The peace you had fought for all your life became a thing of the past. The enlightenment you were supposed to bring to the world didn't happen for many centuries that followed.

"Finally, the Kingdom Ling dissolved into smaller states, and my banishment ended. Since the land was divided into tribes, there was no king. And I was no longer bound by the magic of the realm. But by then, my father had passed away, and I had returned to the Naga realm, never to leave it again.

"My people have been looking for you all this time. But there has never been any news until now."

Until now, those words kept repeating in Gesar's head as he tried to come to terms with everything his mother had told him.

If no one found him, why was he a ghost? And why couldn't he leave the castle where he once ruled as a king? If he was in Deyu when he disappeared, shouldn't he still be there? Where was Deyu in this present world, anyway?

Even after learning so much, all he was left with more questions and no answers. His mother was happy to see him, and he could decide to stay in the Naga realm as she wanted, but he knew he wouldn't do that. He must return to Nur. And he must find out the truth behind his death.

COMING BACK TO LIFE

Nur didn't understand why or how, but for whatever reason, she remembered her past life as if she lived it yesterday, and now centuries ago. That wasn't important, though. The crucial thing was to find Gesar and make him remember his past because he needed to recall how he died.

She knew now why she felt drawn to the castle. Finally, she understood the choices she must make. And she would do it happily.

To think, he waited centuries to discover the truth. How he must have suffered? Nur sobbed as her hands clutched the steering wheel tighter. Her body shook with each sob, and her breath hitched with each shake.

She had killed him. Oh, she understood that she might not have stabbed him herself, but her foolishness had caused his demise. If only she had thought clearly and considered her actions before waging a war she couldn't possibly win. Things would be different. Gesar would have lived and died in old age. Just like he was supposed to.

If Jiacha hadn't lied and told her the truth about the curse, she would have looked for the cure instead of fighting demons. But he was a weak man easily swayed by the show of power.

A regretful sigh left her quivering lips. Thankfully, the weather was pleasant, and the roads were empty, or she might have ended up in a ditch driving the way she was.

Parking the car, she grabbed her bag and ran toward the castle. She didn't bother stopping to greet the guards. They were used to her visits and knew she had permission to be there. No one tried to stop her, and she was thankful for that. There was only one thought in her mind: find Gesar and make him remember.

Knowing who Mikal was and what he could do, gave her chills. She must help Gesar move on. Even his ghost wasn't safe anymore. Dead or alive, it wouldn't matter to Mikal. She only hoped he hadn't regained his powers. She knew he had his memories of the past life. She had seen it in his eyes and felt it in his words. No wonder she felt uneasy in his presence and couldn't find the warm-hearted friend she once knew.

On a hunch, she went straight to the east tower. That had always been Gesar's favorite place. They often spent their night there, waiting to welcome the sunrise. The memory brought a smile to her face as she quickened her steps.

She was almost there when someone stepped in front of her, stopping her from continuing her brisk walk toward the tower.

"I knew it," Mikal said, a sneer distorting his features. "You can't resist returning to this damned place, can you? But then, it was your home once. Maybe the past calls to you the way it is calling me."

Nur was out of breath and couldn't reply, but she gave him a hard stare. She wondered how much he recalled and what he planned to do about it.

"But what I don't understand is," he paused dramatically. "Why now and here, of all places?"

Still, she said nothing. He might not know about Gesar's ghost trapped there. And if that were the case, she wanted it to stay that way.

In their past lives, he had killed Gesar. He was a cold-blooded killer who wouldn't hesitate to condemn a soul to wander the earth for eternity. If he realized she could help Gesar to move on, he might try to stop her.

The man standing in front of her wasn't her friend. It wasn't the Mikal of this life, but the demon of their past. The man who was too much of a coward to join the army. The same one who insisted he would bring Gesar back, but instead returned with a lie that broke her heart and became the catalyst for her demise and Gesar's condemnation.

Right before she beheaded Maisa, the woman had confessed to Zhumu how she had cursed Gesar and made him forget his queen. She had told the dying woman all about Jiacha's betrayal. But that wasn't all she had relayed to the distraught queen. She had also told her something no one else knew.

"I know who you are," she said.

Jiacha, and now Mikal, were the reincarnations of the demon god Zanpu. It wasn't the demon king of Deyu who was Gesar's true adversary. It was Jiacha. The wolf in sheep's clothing.

Seeing the truth reflected in the hatred on her face, he shrugged. "I expected nothing less from a seer of your powers."

He circled her as if trying to intimidate her. He failed, though.

"What do you want?"

"Nothing much. I want to know why the memories of my past life have resurfaced now." Then he whispered as if telling her some big secret, "You know, there are only two reasons people remember their past lives if they ever do."

When she didn't bite the bait and stayed quiet, he said, "One, they find their soul mate. Two, they come across their mortal enemy. Which are you, Nur?"

He was thoughtful for a moment. "But no, I have known you for years. If you were the reason behind this remembrance, it would've happened long before now." He looked at her, waiting for response, but she still didn't say anything.

He poked her with his index finger and got right near her face. She could feel his breath on her cheek and resisted an urge to cringe.

Narrowing his eyes, he said, "What do you know?"

"Nothing," she said and realized she had been too quick to answer.

"Ah!" Once again, he circled her invading her space. "I have thought about it. I didn't know right away because I thought I closed that chapter for good. But that's the only explanation."

He stopped pacing and took a step back. One hand on his chin, he drawled, "After all, there's only one person who can trigger both our memories. Your soulmate and my mortal enemy. Has he come back to life, then?"

ONE LAST BATTLE

For the first time in his existence, Gesar understood the meaning of word terrified, because that was how he felt when he looked down from the east tower and saw Nur standing still, while Mikal circled her menacingly like a vulture. He didn't know what they were talking about, but he could tell it was nothing good. Feeling helpless and not knowing how he would help Nur scared him.

And you know what they said about fear, it made you do stupid things. He didn't think twice and jumped from the tower. The fall wasn't going to kill him. Yet, he hadn't anticipated the pain that went through his entire body as if multiple bones were breaking at once. Gritting his teeth, he reminded himself he was dead, and this pain wasn't real. Somehow, mustering up all his strength he stood up and walked toward them.

Gesar marveled at Nur's composure. Unlike him, she wasn't scared of the man. She didn't even blink when Gesar rushed to her side and demanded if everything was okay. Her gaze stayed trained on Mikal. Gesar understood then. She didn't want her friend, who appeared more like an enemy, to know about his ghost.

"Oh, I don't know," she said to Mikal, trying to appear nonchalant. "Maybe he has been reincarnated just like us."

"Impossible."

"Why?"

"Because my dear Nur, to reincarnate you must die first. And Gesar never died."

"What?" Both Gesar and Nur exclaimed.

Of course, Mikal only heard Nur. He laughed as if it was the most amusing thing he had ever encountered. The man seemed to be enjoying himself. And why not? Knowledge was power and he might be the only one of them who knew exactly what happened to Gesar all those centuries ago.

"Shocking, isn't it?" Mikal said, interrupting Gesar's thoughts. "You know what is the most disappointing thing of all?"

When Nur said nothing, he continued, "It's that people have immortalized him in this ridiculous epic, the mighty Gesar of Ling. Can you imagine?"

Once again, Nur remained silent. She observed Mikal as if he was a stranger to her. And Gesar thought he might very well be.

"Ha," Mikal scoffed, continuing with his monologue, "He couldn't defeat me. Technically, he never succeeded in fulfilling his destiny. And yet, history remembers him. But no one has even heard my name. Me? I outwitted the great king Gesar of Ling."

Gesar wanted to laugh at the comical picture Mikal made, but he was too afraid for Nur's safety to do anything other than stare.

Since the moment he had returned from the Naga realm, he had been waiting for her. He knew she would come to see him the first chance she got, and he needed her help to recall the circumstances of his death. And he had also been looking forward to share everything he had learned from his mother.

Pieces were missing from his memory, but he knew Mikal was in his past. Yet, he didn't know what role he played. His thoughts wandered to his half-brother Jiacha, but somehow, he knew that wasn't all. Mikal might be Jiacha's reincarnation but he was more. Otherwise, he wouldn't have been able to hear the snake.

Nur's abilities as a seer were his last hope to fill the gaps in his memory and finally learn the truth behind his murder and the role Jiacha played in it.

He looked at Nur and saw only impatience, not fear. That reassured him and some of the tension left his posture. Though, not all because he could feel the menace in Mikal's stance. Whether Nur felt threatened of not, Mikal was looking at her as if he wanted to wring her neck. And that scared Gesar.

"Yes, well that's the thing about evil," she said at last, "People tend to forget it as soon as possible. And even when remembered, it's only as a shadow of the good. If Gesar had succeeded in defeating you, your name might have been mentioned in the epic, but only to make him shine brighter. Much like an after thought."

Gesar gave her an incredulous look. What was she doing? Provoking the villain? The woman has no sense of self-preservation. Just because Mikal was once her friend, she was ignoring the fact that the man now standing in front of her wasn't the same Mikal.

"I liked you," Mikal said, unexpectedly. "In the past when you were Zhumu, and even now. But not enough to let you live. In fairness, killing you was never the plan. I just wanted you to forget Gesar and live your life as the queen. I mean, we might have become more than friends."

Nur made a disgusted face and Gesar clenched his fists. This man was getting on his nerves and he wondered what he could do to make him go away. Nothing came to mind, and once again, he was reminded of his helplessness. Being a ghost meant he could do nothing but observe.

"But no, you couldn't accept it and had to fight for your husband. Well, Maisa was your match. The two of you dying like that was a stroke of pure luck, making it so much easier for me to entrap Gesar.

"Ah, and I even managed to evade destiny. He was supposed to defeat me and send me back to the mountain of the damned. When he failed, I lived a long life, and my soul simply returned to the underworld. From there, it was easy for me to reincarnate. A shame it has taken me so many centuries to return to earth, but no matter."

Listening to him, Gesar tried to piece everything together. Something was still missing. Mikal confirmed to be the reincarnation of his half-brother Jiacha, but from what he remembered and what Yelga told him, Jiacha loved him. The brothers were never at odds. He wasn't the enemy. What didn't he know, back then and even now?

"Thank you for the lovely story," Nur said. "It's nice catching up with you. But what do you want from me? Why have you followed me here?"

"I'm not sure, but I feel you might be able to help me. You see, I wasn't always human. Once, I was a demon god terrorizing the heavens and hells. Other gods weren't happy and trapped me in a prison designed for me. But then, for some reason, they decided to reincarnate my soul on earth. Here, I was born as a human and had to rely on others to get what I wanted. Maisa helped, in her way. And so did my human mother, who always had some evil up her sleeves.

"Unfortunately, when I died a human's death my soul didn't return to its original form. And here I am, born as a human yet again. Let's just say, I'm not entirely happy about this situation. I need my powers back, and I'm hoping you might help."

"In case you haven't noticed, I'm also human." She tried to appear bored, but Gesar knew she was becoming impatient. Odd how easily he could read her now that he knew who she was. In his mind, there was no difference between Nur and Zhumu.

"But you are a seer and a powerful one at that. When you went into that trance, you triggered our memories to return. Did you know that? And I'm just wondering what more can you do."

Gesar's heart raced. The man would do anything to get what he wanted. Nur might not be able to help him, but what would he do when he realized she couldn't? In this life, they were friends. Would that matter to the demon god? Only if you could remember.

Frustrated he got closer to Nur, as if that might protect her. And that was when Gesar noticed Nur held something in her right hand. She was trying to give it to him without getting Mikal's attention. He placed his ghostly hand under her clenched fist. She opened it and an object fell into his hand.

It was a small bead of some kind, barely the size of a rice grain. He brought it up to look at the tiny thing. As he looked at it closely, everything faded away. Nur and Mikal vanished from his sight and there was nothing but darkness--emptiness.

'Gods above, what just happened.' But he didn't get a chance to complain or vent to those who playes with human emotions. The world spun and all he could do was to focus on staying upright.

THAT FATEFUL NIGHT

Gesar was back on the east tower, but it was night. the air had a different feel to it-- more homey, somehow. The sky wasn't an inky void but shimmered with stars. His mind was far away, as he paced in anticipation of something good. He didn't understand what was happening, but he had no control over his body or emotions. He felt happy; happier than he had been in years. A thought cane unbidden. He should have sent a message before returning to the palace, but he wanted to surprise Zhumu.

Suddenly, his mind caught up with his surroundings. The war had ended a year ago. He would have returned home at once, but Maisa gave him the potion of forgetfulness, thus cursing him into staying with her. At last, he had broken the curse and returned to his wife. After twelve long years, he would see her again. The elation he felt at the prospect, brought him to his knees.

She appeared then, like a phantom. "You're back."

The statement held no warmth and Gesar wondered why. He tried to hug her, but she resisted. "What's wrong? Aren't you happy to see me?"

Before she could reply, the memory changed and he saw Zhumu holding a sword. And he could do nothing but stare in astonishment as the blade pierced through his heart, and he fell down the tower.

The memory changed yet again and he found himself in a dark place. "Zhumu?" he called out, but there was no reply. He touched his chest and found no hole. His heart ached, though. Not the ache of a sword piercing it, but rather of losing someone he loved.

He was still trying to untangle the web of mystery when he was, once again, back on the tower. This time, it wasn't Zhumu who faced her, but Jiacha. And then, like a mist had been lifted, everything came into focus. He remembered it all.

Those memories of Zhumu and Jiacha were wrong because he had never returned after the final battle with the demon king. His mother had been right and he had stayed in Deyu, cursed to forget everything. He had happily lived with Maisa, thinking her his one true love. But then, Maisa disappeared without telling him anything.

After several weeks, a man came to see him. He hadn't recognized him at the time because of his memory loss. But now, he could see it clearly in his mind. It had been Jiacha. He had forced Gesar to drink something after which everything had turned black.

He didn't know how long he had stayed in the darkness. That part he couldn't recall. But later, he had woken up as a ghost. Not in Deyu, but back at the castle that had always been his home. The place where he had left the one he loved. The one whose embrace he longed for even in death.

△△△

Gesar was back to the present, aware of the truth behind at least one falsehood. All those years ago, when he had awoken as a ghost, he had no memory of his past, but he had always recalled his gruesome death. Yet, he had now discovered that memory wasn't real.

Between the potion of forgetfulness Maisa gave him and whatever potion Jiacha made him drink, his mind had conjured the false memory of meeting Zhumu after twelve years, her betrayal, and his dying at the tower. Those things never happened. But then, what did happen?

Mikal and Nur still faced each other. Nur told him that once he remembered his death, he would be able to move on to the next life. Now what? He recalled everything from his past, but the memory of his death still eluded him.

"Earlier you said," Nur was saying to Mikal, "that Gesar can't reincarnate because he isn't dead. What do you mean by that?"

"I wondered when you would ask me." He smiled and gave her a penetrating look. "If you wish to know the truth, you must find a way to help me return to my demon form. Only then I'll tell you what happened to your beloved."

"Even if I wanted to, I can't. I have no idea how to do that. The only thing I can do is see ghosts and recall the past."

"Too bad then, I guess. Gesar's fate will remain a mystery." He rubbed his hands together as if thinking of something. "I can't let you live, Nur. Unfortunately, you are going to fall down a cliff and die."

Gesar was still holding the bead she had gavin him. He clutched it tightly and for the first time, in a long time, he prayed.

THE OLD MAGIC

A prayer that came from the heart was the oldest magic there was. In desperation, when someone uttered the words to gods, they were always answered. It was an unwritten rule.

Gesar had heard this from his mother and he hoped his prayers would be heard. And it was. Before Mikal could act upon his threat, a group of people appeared as if out of thin air. Just by looking at them, you could tell they weren't of this world.

Their hairs were tired in the same way with golden threads in buns atop their heads. Each wore a different color silk dress, but just as vibrant as the others. Men were barechested and women showed their midriffs. They had all adorned themselves with necklaces and bracelets.

"Your highness, we are here to help," one of them said, and they all bowed to Gesar in unison.

His mother must have been worried about him for her to send the Nagas to Gesar didn't care.

He was glad for their presence. Pointing to Mikal, he demanded, "Cease him," and they wasted no time in grabbing the dumbstruck man and tying him up.

He still couldn't see Gesar and kept shouting for them to release him. While Nur stayed close to Gesar and watched them in fascination.

After some time, Mikal got tired from their lack of response and stopped his wailing. At Gesar's instructions, they took him to the great hall. It was time for good old interrogation.

"It's time to spill the beans," Nur said to Mikal, who was bleeding and cursing on the floor. "Tell me exactly what you did to Gesar and why do you keep saying he's not dead."

As it turned out, The Nagas didn't know the meaning of the word mercy. They used brute force and magic to make him writhe in pain. Yet, the man resisted.

"Why are you making this difficult?" she said again. "You know who these people are. They won't stop until you give them exactly what they want."

"I won't tell you because if you find him, that will be the end of him." As soon as he said the word, he realized his mistake.

"Find him? You mean he is here?" she said.

"No, that's not what I mean," he tried to deny, but it was too late.

Nur knew him well enough to read his

expressions and tell when he lied. Gesar was within the castle walls and perhaps that was why his ghost roamed there.

"He's all yours," she said to the Nagas. Giving Mikal one last disgusted look and leaving his judgment to the Nagas, she and Gesar left in search for his body.

There was no doubt in her mind that he was somewhere in the castle. It all made sense now. The reason why he couldn't leave the place or why he could never move on to the afterlife. It was all because of Jiyach's, or should she say, Zanpu's curse. The demon god had fooled them all.

"Wait," she said. "This place is too big and you have been to every part of it. We won't find anything like this."

"What then?"

"I'll ask for help." Without an explanation, she crossed the corridor and went out into the garden.

Gesar followed her, but she payed him no mind. He watched as she looked around as if searching for the right spot. Finally, she sat down under a tree, closed her eyes, she started chanting something he couldn't understand. The language was unknown to him, and she spoke too softly for him to catch her exact words.

Yet, somethings are universal and by the way she spoke, he guessed she was praying. Her hands were on her knees, palms facing the sky. He could hear her rhythmic breathing. Whatever she was doing, it seemed to be working.

Moments later, she opened her eyes just as a mist appeared and moved towards one of the west buildings. "Let's go," she said, and they followed it.

"What was that all about?" he asked, keeping pace with her.

"I asked my ancestors to send a helping hand." She turned to smile at him, but didn't slow down.

"The mist?"

"They are ghosts of my family. Long gone to the afterlife, yet connected to this world through me. Come on, they knew where they are going."

Across the courtyard, through the corridors, the mist led them to the dungeons. And there, in a small room, at the end of the narrow passageway, they found a crypt.

"Is this it?" he said, more to himself than her. In the castle, it was probably the only place he had avoided like the plague. No wonder the dungeons had creeped him out.

"Moment of truth," Nur said, and opened the crypt to discover his body.

Gesar looked at himself in fascination. The body was well-preserved. If they didn't know any better, they would think he was sleeping. Even his clothes were intact.

"What now?" he said, hoping Nur had an answer because he didn't.

They had found his body and knew he wasn't dead. But his soul was outside the body and as far as he knew, there wasn't a way to return it.

"This is unusual." She seemed to be considering their options. "Maybe your mother can help?"

REUNITED ONCE MORE

It had seemed like a dream to Nur. So much had happened in the short period since she met a ghost in an abandoned castle. When she thought back, the highlight was meeting the Naga people.

"I still can't believe your mother is the Nagi queen," she said to Gesar. The two of them were sitting on a porch swing. "But I'm glad she is. Only she could've helped you reunite with your soul."

He didn't say anything, just hugged her closer to him. Those were some of the scariest moments of their lives. They turned into the happiest, though. That was all that mattered. Since Gesar was back in the world of the living, she had been playing the role of his guide.

The first thing she did, was to buy a small house in Tibet because she knew she could never leave the place. It had always been the home of her heart. Besides, it was the only place where Gesar could live a life of obscurity. In a valley hidden among the Himalayas, no one cared where they came from.

"I don't ever want to let you go," he leaned in and whispered into her hair. "Even an eternity with you won't be enough to make up for the time we lost."

"Let's not think about the past."

The future belonged to them, and they would have ample opportunities to show how much they loved each other.

AFTERWORD

Thank you for reading *Dead Heart Long*, a magical story inspired by the Epic of King Gesar of Ling. I have incorporated the main aspects of the epic and borrowed many names from it, including Zhumu, Jiacha, and Yelga.

The story of King Gesar or Kesar dates back to the 12th century and there are multiple versions of it exist across Central and South Asia, specifically in Tibetan, Mongolian, Buryat, Balti, Ladakhi, Monguor, Yugur, Salar, as well as, among Altai, Turkic, and Tungus tribes. The stories are often told through a blend of poetry and prose. So, you might imagine why I find it fascinating.

The epic is extensive and includes stories that are as old as time. I sincerely hope you enjoyed this tale, encompassing ancient myths, legends, and cultural elements of different regions and generations.

I wrote *Dead Heart Longing* for the Immortal's

Conquest 2022 and it was the grand winner of the same. Categorized as Asian Fantasy, it invites readers to explore realms where reality blends with the otherworldly, where courage battles fate, and where the heart's longing knows no bounds.

For me, this work holds a special place because it made me work outside of my norm and explore cultures that were new to me. I hope the story lingers in your mind long after you close the book.

Once again, thank you for joining me on this journey.

Warm regards,

Dr. Fizza Younis

ABOUT THE AUTHOR

Fizza Younis

Dr. Fizza Younis resides in the vibrant city of Lahore, Pakistan, where her journey through life has been as diverse as the tapestry of her country. With a Ph.D. in economics, she has delved deep into the intricate webs of financial theory, but it's the enchanting realms of fiction and poetry that have captured her heart. As a dedicated indie author and ardent reader, she revels in the art of storytelling, crafting narratives that transcend the boundaries of her academic pursuits. Rooted in the principles of minimalism, equality, and harmony, her writing reflects her steadfast beliefs. Her stories are both mirrors of her philosophy and windows into the lives of intriguing characters navigating the labyrinth of existence. In her world, characters come alive, and their misadventures resonate with the shared joys and tribulations of humanity. With every word, she sprinkles love and encouragement, creating a cocoon of empathy and connection that envelops her readers. Though she might describe herself as an average person leading a mundane existence, in the world of fiction, Fizza is nothing short of spectacular. Join her on a journey through the written word, where ordinary lives take on extraordinary hues, and the essence of humanity is distilled into every sentence.

BOOKS BY THIS AUTHOR

Novella

Dream Within Dream

Short Stories

Words & Wishes
Demons & Dreams
The Life I've Lived

Short Story Collection Books

Soul Seeks the Truth
When Love Fails
Monsters & Mysteries
Tell Me a Fairytale
Dear Earth With Love: & Other Stories

Fairytales With A Twist (Retellings)

Somewhere in Time
The Mirror
Through Time

Poetry Collection Books

Depths Untrodden
No Word Unsaid

Upcoming

Myths of the Night

Collaboration

Cross-Strings (An Interactive Novel)

Made in the USA
Middletown, DE
03 April 2024